j398.2   c.1
GRI

Grimm
    The goose girl ; a new
translation illustrated by
Marguerite de Angeli

BRUMBACK LIBRARY

3 3045 00074 7549

CHILDREN'S DEPARTMENT
THE BRUMBACK LIBRARY
OF VAN WERT COUNTY
VAN WERT, OHIO

D1088295

275
Up to 10
GR 1-5

THE GOOSE GIRL

Other Books by Marguerite de Angeli

BLACK FOX OF LORNE

BOOK OF NURSERY AND MOTHER GOOSE RHYMES

BOOK OF FAVORITE HYMNS

BRIGHT APRIL

COPPER-TOED BOOTS

THE DOOR IN THE WALL

ELIN'S AMERIKA

HENNER'S LYDIA

JARED'S ISLAND

JUST LIKE DAVID

THE OLD TESTAMENT

PETITE SUZANNE

A POCKET FULL OF POSIES

SKIPPACK SCHOOL

TED AND NINA GO TO THE GROCERY STORE

THEE, HANNAH!

YONIE WONDERNOSE

THE GOOSE GIRL

a new translation illustrated by

Marguerite de Angeli

j398.2
GRI

DOUBLEDAY & COMPANY, INC.   GARDEN CITY, NEW YORK

Library of Congress Catalog Card Number 64-10043
Copyright © 1964 by Marguerite de Angeli
All Rights Reserved
Printed in The United States of America
First Edition

*This old folk tale was rewritten from the
Grimm collection. It is dedicated to our
thirteen grandchildren—*

Nina

*who helped me with the translation from the
German, and who is the eldest; her brother*

Anthony de Angeli

David, Jeffrey & Henry Kuhn

Kate de Angeli

Sarah, Dailey & Thomas de Angeli

Michael, Peter, Daniel & John de Angeli

—with my love,

Marguerite de Angeli

10/29/64   mcc ce

C. 1

Once, there lived a Queen who, though she was not very old, felt the weight of years. She had lost her husband long ago and had promised to send her only daughter to a far country to marry a prince. The Queen loved her daughter dearly, and when it was time for departure, there was great preparation. Serving women helped to pack her clothing, her jewels, her gold and silver cups, her ribbons and laces, and all the things a royal bride should have. The goods were to be carried on muleback and follow in her train, and a young serving maid was to accompany her and put her hand in that of the prince. The serving maid's horse was an old white nag, sway-backed and spavined. The princess rode her own thoroughbred mare whose name was Falada and who had magic power and could speak.

7

When all was ready, the Queen went to her chamber and, taking a sharp knife, cut her finger, letting three drops of blood fall upon a fine cambric handkerchief. She gave the kerchief to her daughter, saying, "Dear child, keep this carefully, it will be of comfort to you in case of need on your journey."

The princess tucked the kerchief in her bosom and bade her mother a sorrowful farewell. Then she mounted Falada and set out with the serving maid for her bride-

groom's country. The sun was warm and when they had ridden for a time, the princess said, "Please get down and fetch me some water from yonder stream in my golden cup."

But the serving maid had grown bold since leaving the Queen's household. She said, "I am no longer your servant. Get down and drink from the stream if you are thirsty." In her great thirst the princess dismounted, lay down beside the water, and drank. "Alas!" she said, and the drops of blood answered, "If your mother knew this it would break her heart."

The lovely young princess was humble and said nothing, thinking perhaps she had been too demanding. She mounted Falada and they set off again.

When they had ridden some miles farther, the sun was at high noon and piercing hot. The princess again became very thirsty, and when they reached a brook she called out once more to her serving maid.

"Please get down and fetch me a drink in my golden cup," forgetting how rudely she had been answered before. The serving maid was more haughty than ever.

"Get down and drink if you are thirsty," she said. "I am not your servant."

Because she was so very thirsty the princess dismounted, and, kneeling by the brook, she cried, longing to be back with her dear mother.

"Ah, me!" she wept, and the drops of blood answered, "If your mother knew this it would break her heart."

While she stooped to drink, the kerchief with the three drops slipped out of her bosom and fell into the flowing stream. In her distress she did not notice that it floated away. But the sly serving maid saw it. She knew now that she had the princess in her power, for no longer would the drops of blood comfort her.

As the princess was about to mount Falada, the serving maid said, "By rights, Falada belongs to me. Here, you can have this jade."

The poor young princess was now afraid of the wicked serving maid and handed over the reins. Then, in a harsh voice, the maid ordered her to take off her fine clothes and put on the mean garments of a servant. Finally she forced her mistress to kneel and swear by heaven that she would not tell a single soul at court what had taken place. Otherwise she would be killed.

Falada saw all but kept her own counsel. The serving maid put the real bride on the old white nag and mounted Falada herself. They continued their journey through the afternoon, cooler now that the sun was low.

12

There was great rejoicing when they arrived at the castle. The prince came forth to welcome them and lifted the serving maid from her horse, thinking she was his bride. She was led upstairs, but the real princess was left standing below in the courtyard.

14

The old King looked out of the window and saw the fair, delicate creature looking sad and forlorn. He went to the bridal chamber and asked the bride about her companion. Who, he asked, was she?

"Oh," said the false bride, "a poor wench I picked up on the way and brought along for company. Give her something to do to keep her from being idle."

The old King could think of nothing at first. Then he said, "I have a boy who looks after the geese; she may help him."

The boy was called Conrad and the real princess was sent with him to help watch the geese.

Soon after the wedding the false bride said, "Dear husband, I pray you do me a favor."

"That I will gladly," the prince answered.

"Well, then, let the knacker be called to cut off the head of the horse I rode. It was balky on the way and angered me."

Actually, she was afraid the horse would speak and betray her wickedness. So it was settled, and the faithful Falada had to die.

When this came to the ear of the true princess through servants' gossip, she went to the knacker and promised him a gold piece if he would do her a slight service. There was a great dark gateway to the town through which she had to pass every morning and evening. Would he nail Falada's head up in this gateway?

The knacker promised to do as she wished, and when the horse's head was cut off, he nailed it up in the dark

16

gateway. In the early morning when the goose girl and Conrad went through, she stopped and said:

"*Alas, Falada, there thou hangest.*"

And the head answered:

"*Alas! Queen's daughter, there thou gangest.*
   If thy mother knew thy fate,
   Her heart would break with grief so great."

Then they passed on out of the town right into the fields with the geese. When they reached the sunny meadow, the princess sat in the grass and let down her hair. It shone like pure gold, and when Conrad saw it he was so delighted that he wanted a strand to hold. But the princess said:

"*Blow, blow little breeze*
   And Conrad's hat seize,
   Let him fly to the chase
   And away he will race,
   While I my hair twine
   With its ribbon so fine."

A strong wind came up. It blew Conrad's hat off and

across the fields. He had to run so far after it that when he came back, the princess had finished combing and braiding her hair and the ribbon was tied so he could not get a single strand.

This made Conrad angry. For the rest of the afternoon as they tended the geese he was sulky and didn't say a single word. Even on the way home he walked ahead by himself.

Next morning, when they passed under the gateway, the princess said:

"*Alas! dear Falada, there thou hangest.*"

Falada answered:

"*Alas! Queen's daughter, there thou gangest.*
If thy mother knew thy fate,
Her heart would break with grief so great."

Again, when they reached the meadow, the princess undid her hair and began combing it. Conrad ran to pull out a golden strand, but she said quickly:

21

"Blow, blow little breeze,
And Conrad's hat seize,
Let him fly to the chase
And away he will race,
While I my hair twine
With its ribbon so fine."

The wind sprang up as before and blew Conrad's hat far, far across the field, and he had to go after it. When he came back, the hair was all in place in long braids and not a single hair could he pull out. They tended the geese till evening.

When they got home to the castle, Conrad went to the old King and said, "I won't tend the geese with that goose girl again."

"Why not?" asked the King.

"Oh, she vexes me every day."

The old King then ordered Conrad to tell what it was she did to vex him so.

"In the morning," he said, "when we pass under the dark gateway with the geese, she talks to a horse's head that hangs on the wall. She says to it:

"Alas! Falada, there thou hangest."

And the head answers:

"Alas! Queen's daughter, there thou gangest.
If thy mother knew thy fate,
Her heart would break with grief so great."

Then Conrad told the King all that happened in the meadow when the maiden called up a wind and made him run after his hat while she combed her golden hair.

The old King bade Conrad to go out next day as usual, then placed himself behind the dark gateway and heard the princess speaking to Falada's head. He followed into the field and hid himself behind a bush. He saw the goose girl sit down in the grass with the geese around her; after a time she let down her hair, which glistened in the sun, and he heard her say:

"*Blow, blow little breeze*
And Conrad's hat seize,
Let him fly to the chase
And away he will race,
While I my hair twine
With its ribbon so fine."

Then came a puff of wind which carried off Conrad's hat, so he had to run after it. While he was away, the princess combed and braided her hair. All this the King watched, then slipped away unnoticed.

In the evening when the goose girl came home, he called for her to come to him and asked why she did all these things.

"That I may not tell you," she answered sorrowfully, "nor any living creature, for I have sworn an oath under the open sky. Had I not done so, I should have lost my life."

The old King pressed her sorely and gave her no peace, but he could get nothing out of her. At last he said, "If you will not tell me, unburden yourself to the fire place." Then he left her.

The poor child crept up to the hearth and, beginning

to weep and lament, told all that was in her heart. "Here am I, forsaken by all the world," she said, "yet I am a Queen's daughter. My false serving maid brought me to such a pass that I had to take off my royal robes and put on hers. She took my place with my bridegroom and I have to do service as a goose girl. If my mother knew it, it would break her heart."

The old King stood outside near the chimney and heard all that she said.

He came back and told the princess to go to her chamber in the castle wall. Then he sent royal robes to be put upon her and her beauty was a marvel.

The old King called his son and told him about the false bride; that she was only a serving maid, but here was the true bride whom they had called the goose girl.

27

The young prince was charmed with her youth and beauty. A great feast was prepared to which all the courtiers and friends were bidden. The bridegroom sat at the head of the table with the princess on one side and the serving maid on the other. But the serving maid didn't recognize the princess because of her dazzling apparel and the new way her hair was fashioned.

28

When they had eaten and drunk and all were merry,
the old King put a riddle to the serving woman.

"What does a servant deserve who deceives his mas-
ter?" he asked. Then he recounted the whole story as he
had heard it when he listened at the chimney. When the
King had finished the tale he ended by asking "Tell me,
what doom does such a servant deserve?"

29

The false bride spoke. "No better than this. She must be put stark naked into a barrel stuck with nails, and be dragged along by two white horses from street to street till she is dead."

"Then that is your own doom," said the King, "and your judgment shall be carried out."

And so it was.

Then the young prince married his true bride and so at last the goose girl became a queen. When the old King died the young couple ruled their kingdom nobly, walking in peace among their subjects and living in happiness ever after.

ABOUT THE AUTHOR

Marguerite de Angeli's warm and wonderful talent has delighted young readers since the publication of her first book in 1935. Mother of five herself, and grandmother of thirteen, Mrs. de Angeli has always done much of her work from live models. She was born in Lapeer, Michigan, and moved to Philadelphia, Pennsylvania (where she now lives), as a child.

Over the years, nineteen of her books have found their way from her heart to the hearts of children all over the world, and this book, like her others, is testimony to the joy in living she is able to share with her readers. In 1950 Mrs. de Angeli was awarded the Newbery Medal for *The Door in the Wall,* as the most distinguished contribution to American literature for children of that year.